Series 401
A Ladybird Book

THE GREEN UMBRELLA provides pleasure and excitement for Timmy and Bluebell and their many little bunny friends on the sea-shore. Their frolics and Bluebell's adventurous ride are charmingly illustrated and descriptively told in verse.

THE GREEN UMBRELLA

Story and illustrations by
A. J. MACGREGOR

Verses by W. PERRING

Ladybird Books Loughborough

Once upon a time a Bunny

    Lived beside the deep blue sea,

Once upon a sunny morning

    " Lovely for a swim ! " said he.

Timmy ran to tell the others,
    Having breakfast down below,
" Hurry up, it's grand for swimming !
    Come on, boys, you're very slow ! "

So they gobbled up their breakfasts,
    —And they gobbled much too fast—
Bluebell Bunny, always hungry,
    Nearly always finished last.

Off they went to Cousin Mary's

—Mary lived at No. 10—

Found the house was shut and silent,

Banged upon the door and then—

Went inside . . . Oh, what a bedful!

What a bunch of Bunny-boys!

What a row of ears and noses!

And the snoring—what a noise!

Timmy pulled the bedclothes from them,

  Startled bunnies stared at him,

And a row of ears uplifted

  Heard him say '' Come on and swim !

Then they went to Cousin Mary,

    Told her what they wished to do,

(Bluebell's mind was still on breakfast,

    And she found the carrots, too!)

At the cupboard Cousin Mary

Looked for something nice to eat,

While the little bunnies watched her

Hoping there'd be something sweet.

Then she packed a lovely basket,

　　Sandwiches and slabs of cake,

Bread and jam and juicy apples,

　　—Bluebell thought "Am I awake?"

Tim could hardly lift the basket

    Packed with such a lovely feast,

" Why," he said " we've tons of apples

    —Anyway, a pound at least."

Bluebell gazed upon the basket,

    Said " I'll help you with the food,

Two of us will make it easy,"

    Tim said "All right, if you're good ! "

Off they went across the sea-shore,

　　Waving spades with shouts of glee,

Then they saw the green umbrella,

　　Said " Whatever can it be ! "

" Look, boys ! It's a green umbrella ! "

Ricky said " Let's open it ! "

And they did, with quite a struggle,

" Now let's find a place to sit."

Underneath their green umbrella,

Like a tent, they sat at last,

Timmy tied his spotted hanky

Like a flag upon a mast.

" Now " said Timmy, " Lunch is ready ! "

—Much to Bluebell's great delight—

And the row of hungry bunnies

Really was a happy sight.

Timmy said, when lunch was ended,

    " Some can paddle, some can swim ! "

Off came shoes and coats. But Bluebell

    Said " I'd rather sit here, Tim."

Tim said " Oh, you are a baby ! "

Led them down towards the sea,

With the ball. The others followed.

" Ricky, can you catch ? " said he.

Bluebell came and tried the water,

Touched it with her little toe !

Found it much too cold, and said so,

Back the baby had to go.

But beneath the green umbrella,

Bluebell didn't mind at all,

She was busy with an apple,

" Let them play at silly ball ! "

Everyone was very happy,

    Till they heard a sudden shout,

Saw the green umbrella blowing,

    Up and down and round about.

Bluebell, clinging to the handle

    Bumped and rolled upon the beach,

Everybody ran to save her

    But she floated out of reach.

Up it sailed, the green umbrella,

Up and out towards the sea;

Bluebell held the handle grimly,

Thinking " I'll be late for tea ! "

Open-mouthed the other bunnies

    Watched her sailing overhead,

Held their breath and watched her sadly,

    " Bluebell will be drowned ! " they said.

Floating in the green umbrella,

 Bluebell thought it rather fun;

Wasn't much afraid of drowning,

 But, she thought, she'd like a bun.

Shorewards came the green umbrella,
    Gently floating on the tide,
Timmy used his spade to pull her:
    Bluebell said " That *was* a ride ! "

Soon packed up, they wandered homeward
    Leaving sun, and sand and sea,
And a lonely green umbrella !
    (Bluebell thought " Hurray for tea ! ")